This book
Belongs + o:
trevor

To Christian, who gave me the idea.
— M. B.

To my dad, William F. Hobbie.
— L. C.

ISBN 0-439-67045-4

Copyright © 2006 by Matt Berry. Illustrations © 2006 by Lucy Corvino.
All rights reserved. Published by Scholastic Inc.
SCHOLASTIC, CARTWHEEL BOOKS, and associated logos
are trademarks and/or registered trademarks of Scholastic Inc.

Library of Congress Cataloging-in-Publication Data is available.

Book design by Keirsten Geise
Printed in Singapore 46 • First printing, June 2006

Visit scholastic.com for information about our books and authors online.

Up on Daddy's Shoulders

by Matt Berry

Illustrated by Lucy Corvino

SCHOLASTIC

New York Toronto London Auckland Sydney
Mexico City New Delhi Hong Kong Buenos Aires

Up on Daddy's shoulders,
I am bigger than my big ~~brother~~.
cousin

Up on Daddy's shoulders,
I'm even taller
than my ~~grandfather~~.
morfar

Up on Daddy's shoulders,
I can *bam*!
jam!
slam-dunk
the basketball.

Up on Daddy's shoulders,
I am as big as our great big house.

Up on Daddy's shoulders,
I can see over all the rooftops.

Up on Daddy's shoulders,
I can touch
the tops of the trees.

Up on Daddy's shoulders,
I can fly like a bird on a breeze.

Up on Daddy's shoulders,

I am taller than the giraffe at the zoo.

Up on Daddy's shoulders,
I'm bigger than
the stilt walker, too.

Up on Daddy's shoulders,
I can soar above the hills
and the clouds.

Up on Daddy's shoulders,
I can touch
the moon
and the stars.

Up on Daddy's shoulders,
I'm the happiest kid in the world.